The Rumor Report

The Big Jump

Two Plays

by Staci Swedeen
illustrated by John Martin

Table of Contents

Focus on the Genre: Plays 2

Tools for Readers and Writers 4

Dramatic Literature 5

The Rumor Report 6

The Big Jump 16

The Writer's Craft: Plays 30

Glossary 32

Make Connections Across Texts . . . . . . Inside Back Cover

What is a play?

A play is a story written in script form (words for actors to say and stage directions). The main goal is the script is performed by actors in front of an audience. Some people enjoy reading plays in the same way that they read a story, though the format is different. The events in a play are shown in short sections called scenes. The scenes may be grouped into larger sections called acts. Many plays are divided into two or three acts. Plays consist almost entirely of dialogue—conversation between people.

What is the purpose of a play?

A play shows people in action. The main characters face a conflict or have a problem to solve. The purpose of a play is to let the audience (or reader) connect with the characters in the story and experience their emotions. The audience has a chance to share the characters' successes or failures, and to feel the same fear, love, hope, joy, and other emotions that the characters feel as the play develops.

How do you read a play?

Part of the fun of reading a play is getting to know the characters. They are usually described in a section that precedes the play. Pay careful attention to the dialogue. Nearly all of the information about the characters and the plot comes from what the characters say and do. Then note the setting, when and where the story takes place. When reading a play, you need to use your imagination to "see" the settings and actions as described by

- Plays usually have one or more main characters and additional minor characters.
- Plays are written to be performed by live actors, onstage.
- Plays are told through dialogue and characters' actions.
- The play's plot is based on conflict— a problem for the character to solve or a decision to make.
- Play scripts include stage directions.
- Plays take place in one or more time frames and settings.
- Plays may be divided into scenes or acts.

the playwright. Finally, there are notes to the actors, director, and designers called stage directions. Stage directions are written within parentheses. As you read, you will find it helpful to picture who is talking, who is listening, who is onstage, and who is not.

Who invented plays?

The ancient Greeks performed the earliest plays. They came up with the idea of an actor who speaks and acts, or "plays at" being someone else. These early plays influenced future authors of plays, whom we call playwrights (*wright* means "maker"). Centuries later, one of the world's most famous writers, William Shakespeare, wrote many plays that are still read and performed.

Idiom

An **idiom** (IH-dee-um) is a phrase or expression that makes language more colorful and interesting. Idioms do not use the literal (exact) meaning of the phrase. Consider this exchange of dialogue from a play:

Robin: I'm really tired. How about we work on this project tomorrow?

Steve: Robin, **you really need to pull your own weight**. Otherwise, we'll never finish building this atom model.

In the literal sense, this phrase means that Robin pulls an object equal to how much she weighs. When used as an idiom, it means someone who is not doing her fair share of the workload. Playwrights include idioms to give their dialogue a natural, everyday feel because they reflect how people really talk.

Prefixes

Prefixes are small letter groups added at the beginning of a base word or root that change the meaning of the word. Understanding prefixes and their meanings helps readers and writers build vocabulary. Simple prefixes include **un-**, meaning "not," and **re-**, meaning "again." More advanced prefixes include **syn-**, meaning "together"; **magni-**, meaning "great"; and **pan**, meaning "all."

Make Inferences

Good authors don't explain everything in a story. Often, authors provide clues and evidence in their texts and expect the reader to "read between the lines," or make inferences. Good readers consider the information an author provides and think about other truths the information suggests. To make an inference, look for parts of the text that make you stop and think to yourself, *I wonder if the author is saying that . . .*

Dramatic Literature

Plays are a type of literature called drama. Drama falls into two broad categories: Comedies are funny and usually have a happy ending. Tragedies are serious and have an unhappy ending.

Plays were the first dramatic literature. They go back thousands of years.

FAMOUS COMEDIES

FAMOUS TRAGEDIES

Movies are another type of dramatic literature, but they are only about 100 years old.

TV shows, including situation comedies, animated cartoons, mysteries, adventures, and soap operas, are also forms of dramatic literature. Television, however, became popular only in the 1950s.

The Rumor Report

Cast of Characters

(in order of appearance)

MARISA: Kate's best friend. Pretty and popular, she is stylish in a flamboyant way.

KATE: A high school sophomore who wants to fit in. She wears conservative clothes.

JOSH: A junior, Josh is the captain of the basketball team. Tall, good-looking, not as arrogant as he could be.

MEL: The class clown. He and Josh have known each other since childhood.

Setting

The hallway lockers at Pleasantdale High School, Friday, 11:30 A.M.

(The loud ringing of a class bell is followed by the sounds of students heading off to class. Lights up on a row of lockers in a hallway at a suburban high school. KATE'S locker door is open. It is filled with books and papers. MARISA is wrapping a blue shawl around KATE'S shoulders. They are in the middle of an animated conversation.)

MARISA: Oh, that looks **magnificent** on you! It brings out the blue in your blue eyes. You should wear bright colors more often, Kate. People will notice you.

KATE: No one ever notices me. Everyone just thinks I'm that nerdy girl in Calculus. I don't know what I would do if you weren't my friend, Marisa. *(pause)* Do you really think this brings out the blue in my eyes?

MARISA: Absolutely. My mom said these shawls were such a steal that she bought two of them—one red, one blue. Hey, you know what would be cool? If we each wear one to the dance! *(KATE takes the shawl off and hands it back to MARISA.)*

KATE: I won't be going to the dance.

MARISA: Why not?

KATE: You know why not—because no one ever asks me.

MARISA: There's still plenty of time. The dance isn't until next Friday!

KATE: You keep forgetting that I'm not like you. You wear super-cool clothes. You're funny and popular. People like to be around you. I don't know how you do it.

MARISA: First off, don't be so shy! Guys will think you're stuck-up. You have to be willing to talk and be a good sport and share your lunch. Stuff like that. Oh wait! I forgot my lunch in the classroom. Be right back! *(MARISA runs off. KATE sighs and turns back to her locker. She attempts but is unable to reach a book at the very top. JOSH enters.)*

Josh: Let me get that for you.

Kate: Oh, Josh! Hi!

Josh: I'm used to reaching stuff on the top shelves. Little old ladies ask me to help them all the time at the supermarket, and then they say, "You must be on the basketball team!" And I say, "Yeah, I'm the captain."

(JOSH *hands* MARISA'S *book to her.*)

Josh: This is like fate. I was looking for you and then—boom! I ran into Marisa. You two hang out together, right?

Kate: Right, we—wait. *(excited)* Did you say you were looking for me?

Josh: I want to ask you something. You're so quiet in class that I feel kind of funny about it.

Kate: You don't think I'm stuck-up or anything, do you? 'Cause I'm not. Really. I'm paying attention, that's all. *(thrilled)* So . . . what do you want to ask?

JOSH: Well . . . I got home really late last night and I didn't have time to finish the homework for Mr. Wagner's Calculus class. If I don't turn it in, I think he might flunk me. Can I borrow yours?

KATE: (*disappointed*) That's what you wanted to ask me?

JOSH: Yeah. Can I?

KATE: (*conflicted*) It was hard. The last part took me forever. I . . . I don't know.

JOSH: Come on, what do you say? Be a sport. I'll owe you big-time, Kate.
(KATE *thinks about this for a few seconds, somber, then smiles and hands* JOSH *the homework.*)

JOSH: Great! You're saving my life! I promise I'll get it back to you before class.
(JOSH *exits.* MARISA *runs back onstage eating an apple.*)

MARISA: I ran into Josh and he told me he had something very important to ask you! Did he ask you out?

KATE: No.

MARISA: What did he want, then?

KATE: To borrow my homework.

MARISA: No! You didn't let him, did you?
(*Pause.* KATE *looks uncomfortable but doesn't reply.*)

MARISA: I don't believe it! You could get in a lot of trouble. How come whenever I've been totally desperate and begged you for homework, you never gave it to me? And I'm your best friend!

KATE: Didn't you just tell me that I need to share to be popular?

MARISA: Your homework? Are you serious?

KATE: I know, I know, it goes against my "no moochers" policy. It's not like I did something **illegal**. (*pause*) If I tell you a secret, will you promise not to tell anyone?

MARISA: Okay. I promise.

KATE: I thought that maybe if I did something nice for Josh, he would ask me to the dance. I know it's wrong, but I really, really want to go. You have to swear you won't say a word to anyone about this!

MARISA: I swear, Kate. You can trust me.

(sound of a school bell)

KATE: Look, I've got to go. Catch you later!

(KATE puts the shawl into her locker and then slams it shut and exits. MARISA turns to run off but collides with MEL, who is wearing a backpack.)

MARISA: Watch out where you're going with that backpack! You could kill someone!

MEL: The only way I kill people is with my comedy. Like, what do you call cheese that isn't yours? *(pause)* "Nacho cheese."

MARISA: *Ouch! (changing tack)* Hey, wait—Mel? Mel, come back here for a minute. I want to talk to you.

MEL: Are you finally going to admit that you find me **irresistible**?

MARISA: In your dreams—and my nightmares. You're still good friends with Josh aren't you?

MEL: We have some laughs together. Why?

MARISA: Well, you didn't hear this from me, but . . .

MEL: Go on, Marisa. Spill. I'm all ears. Plus, as you can see, my nose is rather large.

MARISA: Kate just let Josh borrow her homework. She never does that for anyone! I think she really likes him. Does he have a girlfriend now? Has he ever said anything about her to you?

MEL: No, no, and what do you think? That Josh and I sit around all day and talk about girls?

MARISA: Well, actually, I think you do! Listen, Kate's a lot of fun. She really wants to go to the dance, and I thought Josh would like to know that she thinks he's cool—that's all. Don't you think they'd make a cute couple?

MEL: *(sarcastically)* I'll make a point to tell him.

(MARISA *exits.* MEL'S *cell phone rings and he answers it.*)

MEL: Hey, Sam. No, I didn't ask her and I'm not going to now. Why? Because that blabbermouth Marisa just told me that Kate's in love with Josh. I know! Always the bridesmaid, never the bride—that's me. It's so unfair. Uh-oh. Speaking of the devil, here he comes. Later. (MEL *hangs up the cell phone as* JOSH *walks on.*)

JOSH: Hey, Mel, did you see Kate?

MEL: No, why?

JOSH: I have something to give her.

MEL: Chocolates? Flowers? A ring?

JOSH: What are you talking about?

(MEL'S *cell phone rings again.*)

MEL: *(on phone)* What? Yeah, Romeo is here—(*to* JOSH) turn around, dude—uh-huh, Cupid's arrow is sticking right out of his backside.

JOSH: Who are you talking to? Who is it?

MEL: No one, nobody—

(JOSH *and* MEL *struggle over the phone until* JOSH *finally ends up holding it.*)

MEL: Hey, man, come on—back off—stop it—don't mess with my phone—

JOSH: *(speaking into the cell phone)* Who is this? Oh, hey, Sam. What?! Who told you that? Mind your own business! (*He hangs up the phone.*) Do you know anything about this? Someone is saying that Kate—

MEL: Yeah, a little bird told me. You two are, like, totally in love now.

JOSH: No way! She was just doing me a favor. It's not a big deal.

MEL: It's a pretty big deal if she gets caught. And she doesn't let anyone else borrow her homework, does she?

JOSH: How do you know about that?

MEL: Word travels. Why are you so upset? Most guys would be happy to have girls falling in love with them right and left. (JOSH *hands the homework papers to* MEL.)

JOSH: *(furious)* You know, Mel, you push things too far sometimes. Here, give these to Kate if you see her. I've got to go. (JOSH *exits.* MEL *takes a marker pen out of his backpack and draws a big heart with the initials "J & K" on the front of* KATE'S *locker. Finishing, he stands in front of the heart as Kate enters.*)

KATE: Hey, Mel, what are you doing?

MEL: Oh, nothing. I just saw Josh. He was in a big hurry so he asked me to give this to you.

12

KATE: Yeah? Thanks.
(MEL *hands her the papers as he steps away from the front of her locker.*)
MEL: And he left you a little note.
KATE: (*embarrassed*) Oh my gosh!
Who put this here?

MEL: You two are quite the item now,
right? I mean, it's pretty obvious—
you gave him your homework,
didn't you?
KATE: Who told you that?!
MEL: Relax. It's no biggie. Hope you have
fun at the dance while I'm home alone.
(MEL *exits as* MARISA *enters.*)
MARISA: Hey, Kate! I have another brilliant idea. If you come
over after school, we can **synchronize** our outfits for the
rest of the week.
KATE: (*exploding*) How could you?! After you promised! I told
you something—a secret—and now the whole school knows!
I could just die!
MARISA: I didn't tell the whole school. Geez. Look, I was just
trying to help you. You're shy, and I thought that if Josh
knew you liked him, he'd ask you out and we could wear
our shawls. Honest, I was just trying to help!
KATE: I will never tell you another thing as long as I live!
Never try to help me—*ever* again! With a friend like you,
who needs enemies?!
(KATE *opens the locker, pulls out the blue shawl, and
throws it at* MARISA *before storming off. Another class
bell rings. Blackout.*)

The End

Analyze the Characters and Plot

- Who are the characters in the play?
- Where does the play take place?
- What is the main problem in the play?
- How is the problem resolved? Or is it resolved?
- What happens at the end of the play?

Focus on Comprehension: Make Inferences

- Kate has probably never been to a dance. How can you tell?
- Marisa is not as good a student as Kate. How can you tell?
- What information in the play suggests that Mel likes Kate?

Analyze the Tools Writers Use: Idioms

- What does Marisa mean when she says the shawls were a steal?
- On page 10, Mel says he's all ears. What does the playwright mean by these words?
- On page 11, Mel says that he's always the bridesmaid and never the bride. Is this a story about weddings? What does that phrase mean?
- Mel tells Josh that a little bird told him about Josh and Kate. Since birds don't talk, what might this idiom mean?

Focus on Words: Prefixes

Make a chart like the one below. For each word, identify its part of speech as it is used in the play. Then identify the word's prefix and the prefix's meaning. Finally, explain how the prefix changes the meaning of the base word or word root.

Page	Word	Part of Speech	Prefix and Its Meaning	How Prefix Changes the Meaning
7	magnificent			
9	illegal			
10	irresistible			
13	synchronize			

The Big Jump

Cast of Characters

(in order of appearance)

 MIGUEL: 24, the guide for The Big Jump zip line canopy tours. Outgoing and athletic, he speaks with a slight Spanish accent.

SAM: 14, David's sensitive younger brother

 DAVID: 16, acts tough to cover his emotions

Setting

A wooden platform high in the trees in the jungles of Costa Rica, late afternoon. The time is the present.

(We hear the high-pitched zipping sound of a metal trolley spinning along a metal cable. This is quickly followed by a loud, masculine scream. Lights up on SAM, DAVID, and MIGUEL, standing on a wooden platform in the rain forest canopy of Costa Rica. SAM and DAVID are anxiously staring out into the forest. They are wearing long pants, T-shirts, and shoes. They also wear helmets, leather gloves, and individual "zip line harnesses"—which wrap around their legs and chest with a hook that allows each individual to be attached to the zip line. MIGUEL is wearing a shirt that says, "Big Jump Canopy Guide." MIGUEL exudes an easygoing, confident, carefree manner.)

In the first stage direction, the playwright sets the scene. She uses sound to establish a sense of place about the world of the play. By beginning in darkness with the zipping sound and loud yell, the playwright focuses the audience's attention toward the action onstage.

Plays are written primarily in dialogue. Dialogue and action are two of the basic techniques playwrights use to reveal character. In addition to establishing the setting as Costa Rica, Miguel's opening lines give clues to his personality: He is a fun, adventurous person who takes this unusual situation in stride. Each character in a play should have a distinct personality and way of expressing himself or herself.

In some instances, playwrights give specific instructions to the actors on how to say their lines and to whom they are directed.

MIGUEL: That was a good yell!

SAM: *(yelling into the forest)* Dad? Are you all right?!

MIGUEL: He's already on the other side of the valley. He can't hear you. But your father has a very loud yell. *Pura vida!* Do you know this expression? It literally **translates** as "pure life"—but here in Costa Rica we use it to mean "cool" or "great" or "this is living!" It's a good thing to yell as you fly through the trees.

SAM: *(angrily turning to DAVID)* Why'd you dare him?

DAVID: I did not!

SAM: What are you talking about? The whole hike up here, you kept complaining about everything. The weather, the food—

MIGUEL: *(to DAVID)* You don't like the food here? Are you serious?
(DAVID *makes a disapproving face as he takes his helmet off.*)

MIGUEL: That is only because you haven't had my black beans and *chicharrones* or my *arroz con pollo.* I'm a very good cook. And my mother's *fresco de fruta—delicioso.*

SAM: Fresco de—?

MIGUEL: *Fruta.* Fruit.

DAVID: Fruit? No thanks.

MIGUEL: Ah, but this is a fruit salad like they make in heaven. Angels weep, it is so good.

DAVID: Look, this whole trip was a stupid idea. We both know why he arranged this "family vacation," Sam.

SAM: At least he's trying to show us a good time.

DAVID: No dice.

SAM: Give him some credit for trying. Instead, you kept ragging on Dad the whole jeep ride up here.

DAVID: He made us come! I didn't want to do a zip line—did you? And all I said was that if he wanted to fly through the trees like a monkey, he should go first.

SAM: You wouldn't let up. You dared him.

DAVID: Yeah? Well, the real reason he went first is because he couldn't wait to get away from you. You're such a baby.

SAM: That's not true! (*yelling into the forest again*) Dad? Hey Dad!

DAVID: Weren't you listening earlier? Miguel said he's too far away to hear us.

MIGUEL: *Sí*, the other side of the jungle. But now it is time for us to join him. *¿Quién es el próximo?* Who goes next? Señor David? Let me check your harness.
(MIGUEL *pulls on* DAVID'S *harness to make sure it's tight enough. It is.*)

MIGUEL: You are good to go. A-OK. Put your helmet back on, let me connect the cable, and then you will be ready to fly.

Every play needs conflict. In addition to having the two brothers arguing over why their father went first on the zip line, the playwright also introduces a mysterious element that makes the reader wonder, *What is the real reason for the family vacation, and why is David so unhappy about it?*

Characters in plays, like real people, have many different sides to their personalities. What does it say about Sam that he rejects the way his brother David portrays him but then immediately calls out for his father? Audience members who make personal connections to the character onstage are more likely to care about them and stay involved in the plot.

DAVID: *(nervously)* Wait a minute, wait a minute.
(DAVID *peers into the distance and then over the side of the platform. He quickly steps back.*)

DAVID: How high up are we, anyway?

MIGUEL: Here? We are at twenty-five meters. About eighty feet.

DAVID: And how far across is it to the other side?

MIGUEL: Five thousand two hundred and three feet. And three inches.

DAVID: Whoa. That's like a mile.

SAM: *(to DAVID)* You scared?

DAVID: I'm not scared.

SAM: So go already.

DAVID: You go.

SAM: No, you go.

DAVID: I wish I could have stayed home instead of being forced to come to Costa Rica and pretend like I'm having fun on a vacation. I can think of about a **billion** other places I'd rather be.

SAM: You ARE scared.

DAVID: I am not!

SAM: Why do you always have to cover up what you're really feeling?

DAVID: Why don't you mind your own business?

SAM: Why don't you jump?

DAVID: Why don't you stop being such an annoying little brother and shut up?

Miguel's goal as tour guide is to get David to use the zip line. David hesitates. This is another obstacle and puts these two characters in a different kind of conflict than the one that exists between the two brothers. By continuing to add pressure to David's situation, the playwright is looking to keep the suspense high and the tension building. Will David jump or not? There is an old saying among playwrights: "Always keep your hero in trouble."

SAM: Mom doesn't like it when you talk to me like that.

DAVID: Yeah, well, I don't see Mom anywhere around here, do you?

SAM: David!

DAVID: Is she over there? Or there? Or over there on the top of the mountain?

SAM: Stop it.

DAVID: So I guess I can talk to you any way I want to!

SAM: You're not funny.

DAVID: I'm not trying to be funny.

SAM: Then what are you trying to do?

DAVID: I'm trying to figure out how to get back down from here and go home and not be a part of this pathetic family.

SAM: What do you mean?

DAVID: Don't act like you don't know what I mean!

SAM: Why do you have to try to ruin everything?

DAVID: Everything's already ruined. When are you going to realize it?

(SAM *throws a punch at* DAVID.)

David: Hey, you little squirt!

(DAVID, *furious, turns to attack* SAM. MIGUEL *intervenes.*)

MIGUEL: *¡Mis amigos!* My friends! No fighting!

SAM: He started it!

DAVID: You crybaby!

SAM: So? At least I'm not afraid to cry!

DAVID: What's the point of crying? She's dead. *(pause)* Mom's dead!

MIGUEL: Hey, hey now! Break it up! Stand apart!
(MIGUEL *gets bottles of water from his satchel and hands one each to* SAM *and* DAVID. *A tense pause as both boys avoid looking at each other and take a drink of water.*)

MIGUEL: We need to cool off. Hydrate. One should never take a big jump when upset. That is a rule of the jungle. This is when mistakes happen and we say things we don't mean. Even the monkeys know this.

DAVID: Does anyone ever not go on the zip line once they're here? You know, like walk back down the mountain?

The verbal conflict continues to build until Sam takes the action of hitting his brother. This physical act escalates the argument into something more serious that causes Miguel to intervene. Plays are about actions that affect other people and cause other actions.

The playwright finally reveals the real reason for David's distress on this vacation. From the beginning of the play, David's behavior has clearly been informed by the death of his mother, but the playwright picked a moment of maximum intensity to reveal it.

MIGUEL: I suppose it has happened, but with me as a guide? Never. All the people on my tour fly back down. (*pause*) Your mother?

SAM: Last year. In a car accident.

DAVID: A drunk driver.

MIGUEL: *Muy triste.* A very sad thing to learn. I'm sorry. *Lo siento.*

SAM: Dad thought it would be good for us to have a change of scenery.

MIGUEL: Ah. *Amigos*, he picked some beautiful scenery. (*pointing out into the jungle*) That tree over there is a mahogany. That one there is a laurel.

DAVID: Big deal.

MIGUEL: It IS a big deal. Look at this **panorama**. Here in Costa Rica, we have many, many trees and they can grow up to 100 feet tall. Your father picked a very good place to come and yell among the trees. And it can be very **beneficial** to yell. Especially out here in the forest, to yell and scream, to let it all out. Like the howler monkeys.

DAVID: Wait. Howler monkeys . . . that's their real name?

MIGUEL: *¡Sí!* Just yesterday I heard one of them yelling—right over there. I think he was yelling at his brother. They were having a fight.

SAM: No way.

23

In real life, humor is often used to diffuse emotionally upsetting situations. Here, the playwright uses humor to change the play's pace and rhythm. Also, Miguel is making a point about David by humorously comparing the quarreling brothers to howler monkeys.

MIGUEL: Yes way. A huge fight.

DAVID: About what?

MIGUEL: I'm not sure. It was hard to figure out because one monkey wouldn't talk.

DAVID: (sarcastically) Yeah, right.

MIGUEL: Listen, man, it's a terrible thing when a howler monkey won't howl. All that howling gets backed up, gets stuck in the lungs and the liver. Constricts the heart. Monkeys can explode from the pressure. It's a terrible thing to witness.

DAVID: You're pulling my leg.

MIGUEL: No, man. I've seen it with my own eyes. *Boom!*

SAM: *Boom?*

MIGUEL: *Boom!* Then monkey guts rain down on you.

DAVID: That's disgusting!

MIGUEL: You're telling me. (*He shivers.*) That's why it's so much better to hear the howling than the silence. When I was younger, my *abuela*—grandmother—and I would sit on the porch and listen to the sounds of the forest. She knew about the plants—all the orchids—and the hummingbirds. If my stomach was upset, she knew the kind of mint plant that would make me feel better. She taught me how to cook my *arroz con pollo*. She was a *persona muy especial*. You know this expression? It means "special person." My *abuela* died when I was about your age—but as long as I remember her and talk about her, she is alive. I think she may be up there—on top of the mountain—still looking down at me. (*pause*) Do you understand what I'm saying to you?

In this monologue, Miguel tells the boys about the death of his own beloved grandmother. Plays will often have a "turning point" in which the main character either accepts or rejects everything that has happened to him or her. How is Miguel's story a turning point for David?

DAVID: Am I supposed to cry?

MIGUEL: No, you're supposed to think . . . about what happens to monkeys when they explode.

DAVID: (*with a small laugh*) Yeah. Okay. I got it.

SAM: Dad's probably wondering what happened to us.

MIGUEL: I'm sure he is. He might even be worried.

SAM: I'll go next.

MIGUEL: Okay, let me check your harness.

DAVID: You can't go before me.

SAM: Why not?

DAVID: Because you're my little brother and I'm older than you, all right? So I gotta go first or it will be total humiliation. I'll never hear the end of it. Besides, I don't want you to steal my thunder.

SAM: Mum's the word.

MIGUEL: David, let me check your harness then, one more time. Good. In the training, we showed you how to break if you want to slow down—remember? You do this?
(MIGUEL *demonstrates a side-to-side motion with his upper arms and body—like a twist.*)

DAVID: I remember. But if I'm gonna go, I want to go fast. And yell. What was that expression again?

MIGUEL: *Pura vida?* Yes. This is living! Adjust your helmet. Here, let me attach the clip to the line.

SAM: *(to DAVID)* You scared?

DAVID: Yes.

SAM: You are?

DAVID: Yes, of course I'm scared! You'd have to be crazy not to be scared. But if Dad can do it, I can do it, so let's stop talking about it and do it, okay?

SAM: Okay!

MIGUEL: Okay! Push off, tuck your legs, and fly through the air.

SAM: Like a howler monkey!

MIGUEL: Ready?
(DAVID *is at the edge of the platform getting into position to jump.*)

DAVID: Ready.

MIGUEL: Set?

DAVID: Oh—wait a minute, wait a minute.

MIGUEL: What?

DAVID: Nothing. Just . . . Sam, you okay with doing this? If you don't want to—I mean, we're family and—

SAM: (cutting him off) I'm right behind you.

DAVID: Good. Okay. Set. On the count of three.

MIGUEL: Uno . . . dos . . . aaaaaand—

MIGUEL and SAM: (yelling together)—GO!!!

(David starts to jump and yells as the lights fade to blackout.)

The End

Throughout the play, David struggles not only with the other characters but also with his own fears and feelings until he is finally forced to acknowledge them. This allows him to take an action that he was unable to do at the beginning—jump. Dramatists work to show characters that develop and change through dramatic action and conflict over the course of the play.

Analyze the Characters and Plot

- Who are the characters in the play?
- Where does the play take place?
- What is the main problem in the play?
- How is the problem resolved?
- What happens at the end of the play?

Focus on Comprehension: Make Inferences

- David has probably not talked very much about his mother's death. How can you tell?
- What can you infer about the vacation thus far?
- What can you infer about Miguel's attitude toward death?

Focus on Symbolism

Symbolism is a literary technique where an object or event has another, deeper meaning. The central event of the play is jumping from a platform and zip-lining through the jungle. That takes courage. But the bigger "jump" of the play is the one David must make to get past his mother's death and move on with his life.

Analyze the Tools Writers Use: Idioms

- What does David mean when he says, "No dice"?
- On page 24, David says, "You're pulling my leg." What does the playwright mean by these words?
- On page 26, David says that he doesn't want Sam to steal his thunder. Thunder can't be stolen. What might this idiom mean?
- Sam tells David, "Mum's the word." The word **mum** comes from the word **mummer**, or **pantomimer**. What does this idiom mean?

Focus on Words: Prefixes

Make a chart like the one below. For each word, identify its part of speech as it is used in the play. Then identify the word's prefix and the prefix's meaning. Finally, explain how the prefix changes the meaning of the base word or word root.

Page	Word	Part of Speech	Prefix and Its Meaning	How Prefix Changes the Meaning
18	translates			
20	billion			
23	panorama			
23	beneficial			

How does an author write a

Reread "The Big Jump" and think about what the playwright did to write this play. How did she develop the characters? The story line? How can you, as a playwright, develop your own play?

1. Decide on a Problem and Conflict

A play is often about a "special" day. It can be an ordinary day, but something important occurs that impacts the life of the main character. In this play, the "special" event, or problem, centers on teenage brothers David and Sam, who are about to ride a zip line through the jungles of Costa Rica during a family vacation. The conflict is between the brothers, but it is also a conflict David is having with himself.

2. Brainstorm Characters

Playwrights ask these questions:

- Who will have a problem in the play? What is my main character like?
- Who will help in the play? What is he or she like?
- What other characters will be important to my play? How will these characters help solve the main character's problem?

Character	Traits
David	angry; afraid; upset; accepting
Sam	concerned; tries to be conciliatory but is brought to anger by his brother; worried; supportive
Miguel	intelligent; friendly; intuitive; good storyteller; wise

3. Brainstorm Setting and Plot

Playwrights ask these questions:

- Where and when does my play take place?
- How will I describe the setting(s)?
- What is the problem of the play?
- What events happen?
- How does the play end?

Setting	a present-day platform high in the trees in the jungles of Costa Rica
Problem of the Story	David is apprehensive about taking his turn zip-lining through the jungle.
Story Events	1. Sam and David argue about who made their father jump first, and the miserable time David is having on the trip. 2. Miguel tries to keep the peace with anecdotes about Costa Rica. 3. David is outfitted to jump next but continues his argument with Sam, finally coming to blows. 4. It is revealed that the boys' mother died recently and that David is still grieving.
Solution to the Problem	Miguel's anecdotes help calm David's fears and more importantly, help him work through his issues about his mother's death. David admits that he is scared, but with Sam's support, he gathers the courage to jump.

Glossary

beneficial   (beh-neh-FIH-shul) helpful; good (page 23)

billion   (BIL-yun) a very large number; 1,000,000,000 (page 20)

illegal   (ih-LEE-gul) against the law (page 9)

irresistible   (eer-ih-ZIS-tuh-bul) impossible to resist (page 10)

magnificent   (mag-NIH-fih-sent) grand; splendid (page 7)

panorama   (pa-nuh-RA-muh) a complete view of an area in every direction (page 23)

synchronize   (SIN-kruh-nize) plan with others to make things happen at the same time (page 13)

translates   (TRANS-lates) turns one language into another language (page 18)